The Runaway Tractor

Heather Amery

Illustrated by Stephen Cartwright

Language consultant: Betty Root
Series editor: Jenny Tyler

There is a little yellow duck to find on every page.

This is Apple Tree Farm.

This is Mrs. Boot, the farmer. She has two children, called Poppy and Sam, and a dog called Rusty.

Ted is the tractor driver.

He has filled the trailer with hay. He is taking
it to the fields to feed the sheep.

Poppy and Sam hear a funny noise.

"Listen," says Sam. "Ted is shouting and the tractor is making a funny noise. Let's go and look."

They run to the top of the hill.

The tractor is racing down the hill, going faster and faster. "It won't stop," shouts Ted.

The trailer comes off.

The trailer runs down the hill and crashes into a
fence. It tips up and all the hay falls out.

The tractor runs into the pond.

The tractor hits the water with a great splash. The engine makes a loud noise, then it stops with a hiss.

Ted climbs down from the tractor.

Ted paddles through the water and out of the pond. Poppy and Sam run down the hill.

Ted is very wet.

Ted takes off his boots and tips out the water.
How can he get the tractor out of the pond?

"Go and ask Farmer Dray to help."

"Ask someone to telephone Farmer Dray," says Ted.
Poppy and Sam run off to the house.

Farmer Dray has a big horse.

Soon he walks down the hill with his horse.
It is a huge carthorse, called Dolly.

Ted helps with the ropes.

Farmer Dray ties the ropes to the horse. Ted ties
the other ends to the tractor.

Dolly pulls and pulls.

Very slowly the tractor starts to move. Ted
pushes as hard as he can and Dolly pulls.

Ted falls over.

The tractor jerks forward and Ted falls in the water.
Now he is wet and muddy all over.

The tractor is out of the pond.

"Better leave the tractor to dry," says Farmer Dray. "Then you can get the engine going again."

Poppy and Sam ride home.

Farmer Dray lifts them onto Dolly's back.
But Ted is so muddy, he has to walk.

Cover design by Hannah Ahmed   Digital manipulation by Nelupa Hussain